C000279443

❝ Sentences to eat with a spoon, and funny like nothing else on earth ❞

**Tilda Swinton**

# A
# WODEHOUSE
*Pick-Me-Up!*

# The Smile that Wins

arrow books

1 3 5 7 9 10 8 6 4 2

Arrow Books
20 Vauxhall Bridge Road
London SW1V 2SA

Arrow Books is part of the Penguin Random House group of companies
whose addresses can be found at global.penguinrandomhouse.com

Penguin
Random House
UK

Copyright © The Trustees of the Wodehouse Estate

'The Smile that Wins' from *Mulliner Nights*, first published in the
United Kingdom by Herbert Jenkins Ltd in 1933
'Jeeves and the Song of Songs' from *Very Good, Jeeves*, first published in the
United Kingdom by Herbert Jenkins Ltd in 1930
'The Great Sermon Handicap' from *The Inimitable Jeeves*, first published in the
United Kingdom by Herbert Jenkins Ltd in 1923
All published by Arrow Books in 2008
This collection first published in the United Kingdom by Arrow Books in 2017

www.penguin.co.uk

www.wodehouse.co.uk

This is a work of fiction. Names and characters are the product of the author's imagination
and any resemblance to actual persons, living or dead, is entirely coincidental.

A CIP catalogue record for this book is available from the British Library.

ISBN 9781787460157

Typeset in 12/14 pt Perpetua Std by Jouve (UK), Milton Keynes
Printed and bound in Great Britain by Clays Ltd, St Ives Plc

MIX
Paper from
responsible sources
FSC® C018179

Penguin Random House is committed to a
sustainable future for our business, our readers and
our planet. This book is made from Forest
Stewardship Council® certified paper.

# CONTENTS

The Smile that Wins                                          1
*In which a little bit of happiness solves
    everything.*

Jeeves and the Song of Songs                               30
*In which Bertie is persuaded to sing, but only
    for a very good cause.*

The Great Sermon Handicap                                  60
*In which, for once, the more verbose the
    vicar, the better.*

# THE SMILE THAT WINS

The conversation in the bar-parlour of the Angler's Rest had turned to the subject of the regrettably low standard of morality prevalent among the nobility and landed gentry of Great Britain.

Miss Postlethwaite, our erudite barmaid, had brought the matter up by mentioning that in the novelette which she was reading a viscount had just thrown a family solicitor over a cliff.

'Because he had found out his guilty secret,' explained Miss Postlethwaite, polishing a glass a little severely, for she was a good woman. 'It was his guilty secret this solicitor had found out, so the viscount threw him over a cliff. I suppose, if one did but know, that sort of thing is going on all the time.'

Mr Mulliner nodded gravely.

'So much so,' he agreed, 'that I believe that whenever a family solicitor is found in two or more pieces at the bottom of a cliff, the first thing the Big Four at

P. G. WODEHOUSE

Scotland Yard do is make a round-up of all the viscounts in the neighbourhood.'

'Baronets are worse than viscounts,' said a Pint of Stout vehemently. 'I was done down by one only last month over the sale of a cow.'

'Earls are worse than baronets,' insisted a Whisky Sour. 'I could tell you something about earls.'

'How about O.B.E.s?' demanded a Mild and Bitter. 'If you ask me, O.B.E.s want watching, too.'

Mr Mulliner sighed.

'The fact is,' he said, 'reluctant though one may be to admit it, the entire British aristocracy is seamed and honeycombed with immorality. I venture to assert that, if you took a pin and jabbed it down anywhere in the pages of *Debrett's Peerage*, you would find it piercing the name of someone who was going about the place with a conscience as tender as a sunburned neck. If anything were needed to prove my assertion, the story of my nephew, Adrian Mulliner, the detective, would do it.'

'I didn't know you had a nephew who was a detective,' said the Whisky Sour.

Oh, yes. He has retired now, but at one time he was as keen an operator as anyone in the profession (said Mr Mulliner). After leaving Oxford and trying his hand at one or two uncongenial tasks, he had found his niche as a member of the firm of Widgery and Boon, Investigators, of Albemarle Street. And it was during his second year with this old-established house that he met and

2

loved Lady Millicent Shipton-Bellinger, younger daughter of the fifth Earl of Brangbolton.

It was the Adventure of the Missing Sealyham that brought the young couple together. From the purely professional standpoint, my nephew has never ranked this among his greatest triumphs of ratiocination; but, considering what it led to, he might well, I think, be justified in regarding it as the most important case of his career. What happened was that he met the animal straying in the park, deduced from the name and address on its collar that it belonged to Lady Millicent Shipton-Bellinger, of 18a, Upper Brook Street, and took it thither at the conclusion of his stroll and restored it.

'Child's-play' is the phrase with which, if you happen to allude to it, Adrian Mulliner will always airily dismiss this particular investigation; but Lady Millicent could not have displayed more admiration and enthusiasm had it been the supremest masterpiece of detective work. She fawned on my nephew. She invited him in to tea, consisting of buttered toast, anchovy sandwiches and two kinds of cake; and at the conclusion of the meal they parted on terms which, even at that early stage in their acquaintance, were something warmer than those of mere friendship.

Indeed, it is my belief that the girl fell in love with Adrian as instantaneously as he with her. On him, it was her radiant blonde beauty that exercised the spell. She, on her side, was fascinated, I fancy, not only by the regularity of his features, which, as is the case with all the Mulliners, was considerable, but also by the fact that he was dark and thin and wore an air of inscrutable melancholy.

This, as a matter of fact, was due to the troublesome attacks of dyspepsia from which he had suffered since boyhood; but to the girl it naturally seemed evidence of a great and romantic soul. Nobody, she felt, could look so grave and sad, had he not hidden deeps in him.

One can see the thing from her point of view. All her life she had been accustomed to brainless juveniles who eked out their meagre eyesight with monocles and, as far as conversation was concerned, were a spent force after they had asked her if she had seen the Academy or did she think she would prefer a glass of lemonade. The effect on her of a dark, keen-eyed man like Adrian Mulliner, who spoke well and easily of footprints, psychology and the underworld, must have been stupendous.

At any rate, their love ripened rapidly. It could not have been two weeks after their first meeting when Adrian, as he was giving her lunch one day at the Senior Bloodstain, the detectives' club in Rupert Street, proposed and was accepted. And for the next twenty-four hours, one is safe in saying, there was in the whole of London, including the outlying suburban districts, no happier private investigator than he.

Next day, however, when he again met Millicent for lunch, he was disturbed to perceive on her beautiful face an emotion which his trained eye immediately recognized as anguish.

'Oh, Adrian,' said the girl brokenly. 'The worst has happened. My father refuses to hear of our marrying. When I told him we were engaged, he said "Pooh!" quite a number of times, and added that he had never heard such dashed nonsense in his life. You see, ever since my Uncle Joe's trouble in nineteen-twenty-eight, father has had a horror of detectives.'

'I don't think I have met your Uncle Joe.'

'You will have the opportunity next year. With the usual allowance for good conduct he should be with us again about July. And there is another thing.'

'Not another?'

'Yes. Do you know Sir Jasper Addleton, O.B.E.?'

'The financier?'

'Father wants me to marry him. Isn't it awful!'

'I have certainly heard more enjoyable bits of news,' agreed Adrian. 'This wants a good deal of careful thinking over.'

The process of thinking over his unfortunate situation had the effect of rendering excessively acute the pangs of Adrian Mulliner's dyspepsia. During the past two weeks the ecstasy of being with Millicent and deducing that she loved him had caused a complete cessation of the attacks; but now they began again, worse than ever. At length, after a sleepless night during which he experienced all the emotions of one who has carelessly swallowed a family of scorpions, he sought a specialist.

The specialist was one of those keen, modern minds

who disdain the outworn formulæ of the more conservative mass of the medical profession. He examined Adrian carefully, then sat back in his chair, with the tips of his fingers touching.

'Smile!' he said.

'Eh?' said Adrian.

'Smile, Mr Mulliner.'

'Did you say smile?'

'That's it. Smile.'

'But,' Adrian pointed out, 'I've just lost the only girl I ever loved.'

'Well, that's fine,' said the specialist, who was a bachelor. 'Come on, now, if you please. Start smiling.'

Adrian was a little bewildered.

'Listen,' he said. 'What *is* all this about smiling? We started, if I recollect, talking about my gastric juices. Now, in some mysterious way, we seem to have got on to the subject of smiles. How do you mean – smile? I never smile. I haven't smiled since the butler tripped over the spaniel and upset the melted butter on my Aunt Elizabeth, when I was a boy of twelve.'

The specialist nodded.

'Precisely. And that is why your digestive organs trouble you. Dyspepsia,' he proceeded, 'is now recognized by the progressive element of the profession as purely mental. We do not treat it with drugs and medicines. Happiness is the only cure. Be gay, Mr Mulliner. Be cheerful. And, if you can't do that, at any rate smile. The mere exercise of the risible muscles is in itself beneficial. Go out now and make a point, whenever you have a spare moment, of smiling.'

'Like this?' said Adrian.

'Wider than that.'

'How about this?'

'Better,' said the specialist, 'but still not quite so elastic as one could desire. Naturally, you need practice. We must expect the muscles to work rustily for a while at their unaccustomed task. No doubt things will brighten by and by.'

He regarded Adrian thoughtfully.

'Odd,' he said. 'A curious smile, yours, Mr Mulliner. It reminds me a little of the Mona Lisa's. It has the same underlying note of the sardonic and the sinister. It virtually amounts to a leer. Somehow it seems to convey the suggestion that you know all. Fortunately, my own life is an open book, for all to read, and so I was not discommoded. But I think it would be better if, for the present, you endeavoured not to smile at invalids or nervous persons. Good morning, Mr Mulliner. That will be five guineas, precisely.'

On Adrian's face, as he went off that afternoon to perform the duties assigned to him by his firm, there was no smile of any description. He shrank from the ordeal before him. He had been told off to guard the wedding-presents at a reception in Grosvenor Square, and naturally anything to do with weddings was like a sword through his heart. His face, as he patrolled the

room where the gifts were laid out, was drawn and for-
bidding. Hitherto, at these functions, it had always
been his pride that nobody could tell that he was a
detective. To-day, a child could have recognized his
trade. He looked like Sherlock Holmes.

To the gay throng that surged about him he paid
little attention. Usually tense and alert on occasions
like this, he now found his mind wandering. He mused
sadly on Millicent. And suddenly – the result, no
doubt, of these gloomy meditations, though a glass of
wedding champagne may have contributed its mite –
there shot through him, starting at about the third
button of his neat waistcoat, a pang of dyspepsia so
keen that he felt the pressing necessity of doing something about it immediately.

With a violent effort he contorted his features into
a smile. And, as he did so, a stout, bluff man of
middle age, with a red face and a grey moustache, who
had been hovering near one of the tables, turned and
saw him.

'Egad!' he muttered, paling.

Sir Sutton Hartley-Wesping, Bart – for the red-
faced man was he – had had a pretty good afternoon.
Like all baronets who attend Society wedding-
receptions, he had been going round the various tables
since his arrival, pocketing here a fish-slice, there a
jewelled egg-boiler, until now he had taken on about
all the cargo his tonnage would warrant, and was
thinking of strolling off to the pawnbroker's in the

Euston Road, with whom he did most of his business. At the sight of Adrian's smile, he froze where he stood, appalled.

We have seen what the specialist thought of Adrian's smile. Even to him, a man of clear and limpid conscience, it had seemed sardonic and sinister. We can picture, then, the effect it must have had on Sir Sutton Hartley-Wesping.

At all costs, he felt, he must conciliate this leering man. Swiftly removing from his pockets a diamond necklace, five fish-slices, ten cigarette-lighters and a couple of egg-boilers, he placed them on the table and came over to Adrian with a nervous little laugh.

'How *are* you, my dear fellow?' he said.

Adrian said that he was quite well. And so, indeed, he was. The specialist's recipe had worked like magic. He was mildly surprised at finding himself so cordially addressed by a man whom he did not remember ever having seen before, but he attributed this to the magnetic charm of his personality.

'That's fine,' said the Baronet heartily. 'That's capital. That's splendid. Er – by the way – I fancied I saw you smile just now.'

'Yes,' said Adrian. 'I did smile. You see—'

'Of course I see. Of course, my dear fellow. You detected the joke I was playing on our good hostess, and you were amused because you understood that there is no animus, no *arrière-pensée*, behind these little practical pleasantries – nothing but good, clean fun, at which nobody would have laughed more heartily than herself. And now, what are you doing this week-end, my dear old chap? Would you care to run down to my place in Sussex?'

'Very kind of you,' began Adrian doubtfully. He was not quite sure that he was in the mood for strange week-ends.

'Here is my card, then. I shall expect you on Friday. Quite a small party. Lord Brangbolton, Sir Jasper Addleton, and a few more. Just loafing about, you know, and a spot of bridge at night. Splendid. Capital. See you, then, on Friday.'

And, carelessly dropping another egg-boiler on the table as he passed, Sir Sutton disappeared.

Any doubts which Adrian might have entertained as to accepting the Baronet's invitation had vanished as he heard the names of his fellow-guests. It always interests a fiancé to meet his fiancée's father and his fiancée's prospective fiancé. For the first time since Millicent had told him the bad news, Adrian became almost cheerful. If, he felt, this baronet had taken such a tremendous fancy to him at first sight, why might it not happen that Lord Brangbolton would be equally drawn to him – to the extent, in fact, of overlooking his profession and welcoming him as a son-in-law?

He packed, on the Friday, with what was to all intents and purposes a light heart.

\*

A fortunate chance at the very outset of his expedition increased Adrian's optimism. It made him feel that Fate was fighting on his side. As he walked down the platform of Victoria Station, looking for an empty compartment in the train which was to take him to his destination, he perceived a tall, aristocratic old gentleman being assisted into a first-class carriage by a man of butlerine aspect. And in the latter he recognized the servitor who had admitted him to 18A, Upper Brook Street, when he visited the house after solving the riddle of the missing Sealyham. Obviously, then, the white-haired, dignified passenger could be none other than Lord Brangbolton. And Adrian felt that if on a long train journey he failed to ingratiate himself with the old buster, he had vastly mistaken his amiability and winning fascination of manner.

He leaped in, accordingly, as the train began to move, and the Earl, glancing up from his paper, jerked a thumb at the door.

'Get out, blast you!' he said. 'Full up.'

As the compartment was empty but for themselves, Adrian made no move to comply with the request. Indeed, to alight now, to such an extent had the train gathered speed, would have been impossible. Instead, he spoke cordially.

'Lord Brangbolton, I believe?'

'Go to hell,' said his lordship.

'I fancy we are to be fellow-guests at Wesping Hall this week-end.'

'What of it?'

'I just mentioned it.'

'Oh?' said Lord Brangbolton. 'Well, since you're here, how about a little flutter?'

As is customary with men of his social position, Millicent's father always travelled with a pack of cards. Being gifted by Nature with considerable manual dexterity, he usually managed to do well with these on race-trains.

'Ever played Persian Monarchs?' he asked, shuffling.

'I think not,' said Adrian.

'Quite simple,' said Lord Brangbolton. 'You just bet a quid or whatever it may be that you can cut a higher card than the other fellow, and, if you do, you win, and, if you don't, you don't.'

Adrian said it sounded a little like Blind Hooky.

'It is like Blind Hooky,' said Lord Brangbolton. 'Very like Blind Hooky. In fact, if you can play Blind Hooky, you can play Persian Monarchs.'

By the time they alighted at Wesping Parva Adrian was twenty pounds on the wrong side of the ledger. The fact, however, did not prey upon his mind. On the contrary, he was well satisfied with the progress of events. Elated with his winnings, the old Earl had become positively cordial, and Adrian resolved to press his advantage home at the earliest opportunity.

Arrived at Wesping Hall, accordingly, he did not delay. Shortly after the sounding of the dressing-gong he made his way to Lord Brangbolton's room and found him in his bath.

'Might I have a word with you, Lord Brangbolton?' he said.

'You can do more than that,' replied the other, with marked amiability. 'You can help me find the soap.'

'Have you lost the soap?'

'Yes. Had it a minute ago, and now it's gone.'

'Strange,' said Adrian.

'Very strange,' agreed Lord Brangbolton. 'Makes a fellow think a bit, that sort of thing happening. My own soap, too. Brought it with me.'

Adrian considered.

'Tell me exactly what occurred,' he said. 'In your own words. And tell me everything, please, for one never knows when the smallest detail may not be important.'

His companion marshalled his thoughts.

'My name,' he began, 'is Reginald Alexander Montacute James Bramfylde Tregennis Shipton-Bellinger, fifth Earl of Brangbolton. On the sixteenth of the present month — to-day, in fact — I journeyed to the house of my friend Sir Sutton Hartley-Wesping, Bart — here, in short — with the purpose of spending the week-end there. Knowing that Sir Sutton likes to have his guests sweet and fresh about the place, I decided to take a bath before dinner. I unpacked my soap and in a short space of time had lathered myself thoroughly from the neck upwards. And then, just as I was about to get at my right leg, what should I find but that the soap had disappeared. Nasty shock it gave me, I can tell you.'

Adrian had listened to this narrative with the closest

attention. Certainly the problem appeared to present several points of interest.

'It looks like an inside job,' he said thoughtfully. 'It could scarcely be the work of a gang. You would have noticed a gang. Just give me the facts briefly once again, if you please.'

'Well, I was here, in the bath, as it might be, and the soap was here — between my hands, as it were. Next moment it was gone.'

'Are you sure you have omitted nothing?'

Lord Brangbolton reflected.

'Well, I was singing, of course.'

A tense look came into Adrian's face.

'Singing what?'

'"Sonny Boy".'

Adrian's face cleared.

'As I suspected,' he said, with satisfaction. 'Precisely as I had supposed. I wonder if you are aware, Lord Brangbolton, that in the singing of that particular song the muscles unconsciously contract as you come to the final "boy"? Thus — "I still have you, sonny BOY." You observe? It would be impossible for anyone, rendering the number with the proper gusto, not to force his hands together at this point, assuming that they were in anything like close juxtaposition. And if there were any slippery object between them, such as a piece of soap, it would inevitably shoot sharply upwards and fall' — he scanned the room keenly — 'outside the bath on the mat. As, indeed,' he concluded, picking up the missing object and restoring it to its proprietor, 'it did.'

Lord Brangbolton gaped.

'Well, dash my buttons,' he cried, 'if that isn't the smartest bit of work I've seen in a month of Sundays!'

'Elementary,' said Adrian with a shrug.

'You ought to be a detective.'

Adrian took the cue.

'I am a detective,' he said. 'My name is Mulliner. Adrian Mulliner, Investigator.'

For an instant the words did not appear to have made any impression. The aged peer continued to beam through the soapsuds. Then suddenly his geniality vanished with an ominous swiftness.

'Mulliner? Did you say Mulliner?'

'I did.'

'You aren't by any chance the feller—'

'. . . who loves your daughter Millicent with a fervour he cannot begin to express? Yes, Lord Brangbolton, I am. And I am hoping that I may receive your consent to the match.'

A hideous scowl had darkened the Earl's brow. His fingers, which were grasping a loofah, tightened convulsively.

'Oh?' he said. 'You are, are you? You imagine, do you, that I propose to welcome a blighted footprint-and-cigar-ash inspector into my family? It is your idea, is it, that I shall acquiesce in the union of my daughter to a dashed feller who goes about the place on his hands and knees with a magnifying-glass, picking up small objects and putting them carefully away in his pocket-book? I seem to see myself! Why, rather than permit Millicent to marry a bally detective . . .'

'What is your objection to detectives?'

'Never you mind what's my objection to detectives. Marry my daughter, indeed! I like your infernal cheek. Why, you couldn't keep her in lipsticks.'

Adrian preserved his dignity.

'I admit that my services are not so amply remuner-ated as I could wish, but the firm hint at a rise next Christmas . . .'

'Tchah!' said Lord Brangbolton. 'Pshaw! If you are interested in my daughter's matrimonial arrangements, she is going, as soon as he gets through with this Bramah-Yamah Gold Mines flotation of his, to marry my old friend Jasper Addleton. As for you, Mr Mull-iner, I have only two words to say to you. One is POP, the other is OFF. And do it now.'

Adrian sighed. He saw that it would be hopeless to endeavour to argue with the haughty old man in his present mood.

'So be it, Lord Brangbolton,' he said quietly.

And, affecting not to notice the nail-brush which struck him smartly on the back of the head, he left the room.

The food and drink provided for his guests by Sir Sut-ton Hartley-Wesping at the dinner which began some half-hour later were all that the veriest gourmet could have desired; but Adrian gulped them down, scarcely tasting them. His whole attention was riveted on Sir Jasper Addleton, who sat immediately opposite him.

And the more he examined Sir Jasper, the more revolting seemed the idea of his marrying the girl he loved.

Of course, an ardent young fellow inspecting a man who is going to marry the girl he loves is always a stern critic. In the peculiar circumstances Adrian would, no doubt, have looked askance at a John Barrymore or a Ronald Colman. But, in the case of Sir Jasper, it must be admitted that he had quite reasonable grounds for his disapproval.

In the first place, there was enough of the financier to make two financiers. It was as if Nature, planning a financier, had said to itself: 'We will do this thing well. We will not skimp,' with the result that, becoming too enthusiastic, it had overdone it. And then, in addition to being fat, he was also bald and goggle-eyed. And, if you overlooked his baldness and the goggly protuberance of his eyes, you could not get away from the fact that he was well advanced in years. Such a man, felt Adrian, would have been better employed in pricing burial-lots in Kensal Green Cemetery than in forcing his unwelcome attentions on a sweet young girl like Millicent: and as soon as the meal was concluded he approached him with cold abhorrence.

'A word with you,' he said, and led him out on to the terrace.

The O.B.E., as he followed him into the cool night air, seemed surprised and a little uneasy. He had noticed Adrian scrutinizing him closely across the dinner table, and if there is one thing a financier who has just put out a prospectus of a gold mine dislikes, it is to be scrutinized closely.

'What do you want?' he asked nervously.

Adrian gave him a cold glance.

'Do you ever look in a mirror, Sir Jasper?' he asked curtly.

'Frequently,' replied the financier, puzzled.

'Do you ever weigh yourself?'

'Often.'

'Do you ever listen while your tailor is toiling round you with the tape-measure and calling out the score to his assistant?'

'I do.'

'Then,' said Adrian, 'and I speak in the kindest spirit of disinterested friendship, you must have realized that you are an overfed old bohunkus. And how you ever got the idea that you were a fit mate for Lady Millicent Shipton-Bellinger frankly beats me. Surely it must have occurred to you what a priceless ass you will look, walking up the aisle with that young and lovely girl at your side? People will mistake you for an elderly uncle taking his niece to the Zoo.'

The O.B.E. bridled.

'Ho!' he said.

'It is no use saying "Ho!"' said Adrian. 'You can't get

out of it with any "Ho's". When all the talk and argument have died away, the fact remains that, millionaire though you be, you are a nasty-looking, fat, senile millionaire. If I were you, I should give the whole thing a miss. What do you want to get married for, anyway? You are much happier as you are. Besides, think of the risks of a financier's life. Nice it would be for that sweet girl suddenly to get a wire from you telling her not to wait dinner for you as you had just started a seven-year stretch at Dartmoor!'

An angry retort had been trembling on Sir Jasper's lips during the early portion of this speech, but at these concluding words it died unspoken. He blenched visibly, and stared at the speaker with undisguised apprehension.

'What do you mean?' he faltered.

'Never mind,' said Adrian.

He had spoken, of course, purely at a venture, basing his remarks on the fact that nearly all O.B.E.s who dabble in High Finance go to prison sooner or later. Of Sir Jasper's actual affairs he knew nothing.

'Hey, listen!' said the financier.

But Adrian did not hear him. I have mentioned that during dinner, preoccupied with his thoughts, he had bolted his food. Nature now took its toll. An acute spasm suddenly ran through him, and with a brief 'Ouch!' of pain he doubled up and began to walk round in circles.

Sir Jasper clicked his tongue impatiently.

'This is no time for doing the Astaire pom-pom

dance,' he said sharply. 'Tell me what you meant by that stuff you were talking about prison.'

Adrian had straightened himself. In the light of the moon which flooded the terrace with its silver beams, his clean-cut face was plainly visible. And with a shiver of apprehension Sir Jasper saw that it wore a sardonic, sinister smile — a smile which, it struck him, was virtually tantamount to a leer.

I have spoken of the dislike financiers have for being scrutinized closely. Still more vehemently do they object to being leered at. Sir Jasper reeled, and was about to press his question when Adrian, still smiling, tottered off into the shadows and was lost to sight.

The financier hurried into the smoking-room, where he knew there would be the materials for a stiff drink. A stiff drink was what he felt an imperious need of at the moment. He tried to tell himself that that smile could not really have had the inner meaning which he had read into it; but he was still quivering nervously as he entered the smoking-room.

As he opened the door, the sound of an angry voice smote his ears. He recognized it as Lord Brangbolton's.

'I call it dashed low,' his lordship was saying in his high-pitched tenor.

Sir Jasper gazed in bewilderment. His host, Sir Sutton Hartley-Wesping, was standing backed against the wall, and Lord Brangbolton, tapping him on the shirt-front with a piston-like forefinger, was plainly in the process of giving him a thorough ticking off.

'What's the matter?' asked the financier.

'I'll tell you what's the matter,' cried Lord Brang-bolton. 'This hound here has got down a detective to watch his guests. A dashed fellow named Mulliner. So much,' he said bitterly, 'for our boasted English hospitality. Egad!' he went on, still tapping the baronet round and about the diamond solitaire. 'I call it thoroughly low. If I have a few of my society chums down to my little place for a visit, naturally I chain up the hair-brushes and tell the butler to count the spoons every night, but I'd never dream of going so far as to employ beastly detectives. One has one's code. *Noblesse*, I mean to say, *oblige*, what, what?'

'But, listen,' pleaded the Baronet. 'I keep telling you. I had to invite the fellow here. I thought that if he had eaten my bread and salt, he would not expose me.'

'How do you mean, expose you?'

Sir Sutton coughed.

'Oh, it was nothing. The merest trifle. Still, the man undoubtedly could have made things unpleasant for me, if he had wished. So, when I looked up and saw him smiling at me in that frightful sardonic, knowing way——'

Sir Jasper Addleton uttered a sharp cry.

'Smiling!' He gulped. 'Did you say smiling?'

'Smiling,' said the Baronet, 'is right. It was one of those smiles that seem to go clean through you and light up all your inner being as if with a searchlight.'

Sir Jasper gulped again.

'Is this fellow – this smiler fellow – is he a tall, dark, thin chap?'

'That's right. He sat opposite you at dinner.'

'And he's a detective?'

'He is,' said Lord Brangbolton. 'As shrewd and smart a detective,' he added grudgingly, 'as I ever met in my life. The way he found that soap . . . Feller struck me as having some sort of a sixth sense, if you know what I mean, dash and curse him. I hate detectives,' he said with a shiver. 'They give me the creeps. This one wants to marry my daughter, Millicent, of all the dashed nerve!'

'See you later,' said Sir Jasper. And with a single bound he was out of the room and on his way to the terrace. There was, he felt, no time to waste. His florid face, as he galloped along, was twisted and ashen. With one hand he drew from his inside pocket a cheque-book, with the other from his trouser-pocket a fountain-pen.

Adrian, when the financier found him, was feeling a good deal better. He blessed the day when he had sought the specialist's advice. There was no doubt about it, he felt, the man knew his business. Smiling might make the cheek-muscles ache, but it undoubtedly did the trick as regarded the pangs of dyspepsia.

For a brief while before Sir Jasper burst onto the terrace, waving fountain-pen and cheque-book, Adrian had been giving his face a rest. But now, the pain in his cheeks having abated, he deemed it prudent to resume the treatment. And so it came about that the financier, hurrying towards him, was met with a smile so mean-ing, so suggestive, that he stopped in his tracks and for a moment could not speak.

'Oh, there you are!' he said, recovering at length. 'Might I have a word with you in private, Mr Mulliner?'

Adrian nodded, beaming. The financier took him by the coat-sleeve and led him across the terrace. He was breathing a little stertorously.

'I've been thinking things over,' he said, 'and I've come to the conclusion that you were right.'

'Right?' said Adrian.

'About me marrying. It wouldn't do.'

'No?'

'Positively not. Absurd. I can see it now. I'm too old for the girl.'

'Yes.'

'Too bald.'

'Exactly.'

'And too fat.'

'Much too fat,' agreed Adrian. This sudden change of heart puzzled him, but none the less the other's words were as music to his ears. Every syllable the O.B.E. had spoken had caused his heart to leap within him like a young lamb in springtime, and his mouth curved in a smile.

Sir Jasper, seeing it, shied like a frightened horse. He patted Adrian's arm feverishly.

'So I have decided,' he said, 'to take your advice and – if I recall your expression – give the thing a miss.'

'You couldn't do better,' said Adrian heartily.

'Now, if I were to remain in England in these circumstances,' proceeded Sir Jasper, 'there might be unpleasantness. So I propose to go quietly away at once to some remote spot – say, South America. Don't you think I am right?' he asked, giving the cheque-book a twitch.

'Quite right,' said Adrian.

'You won't mention this little plan of mine to anyone? You will keep it as just a secret between ourselves? If, for instance, any of your cronies at Scotland Yard should express curiosity as to my whereabouts, you will plead ignorance?'

'Certainly.'

'Capital!' said Sir Jasper, relieved. 'And there is one other thing. I gather from Brangbolton that you are anxious to marry Lady Millicent yourself. And, as by the time of the wedding I shall doubtless be in – well, Callao is a spot that suggests itself off-hand, I would like to give you my little wedding-present now.'

He scribbled hastily in his cheque-book, tore out a page and handed it to Adrian.

'Remember!' he said. 'Not a word to anyone!'

'Quite,' said Adrian.

He watched the financier disappear in the direction of the garage, regretting that he could have misjudged a man who so evidently had much good in him. Presently the sound of a motor engine announced that the other was on his way. Feeling that one obstacle, at least, between himself and his happiness had been removed, Adrian strolled indoors to see what the rest of the party were doing.

It was a quiet, peaceful scene that met his eyes as he wandered into the library. Overruling the request of some of the members of the company for a rubber of bridge, Lord Brangbolton had gathered them together at a small table and was initiating them into his favourite game of Persian Monarchs.

'It's perfectly simple, dash it,' he was saying. 'You just take the pack and cut. You bet – let us say ten pounds – that you will cut a higher card than the feller you're cutting against. And, if you do, you win, dash it. And, if you don't, the other dashed feller wins. Quite clear, what?'

Somebody said that it sounded a little like Blind Hooky.

'It is like Blind Hooky,' said Lord Brangbolton. 'Very like Blind Hooky. In fact, if you can play Blind Hooky, you can play Persian Monarchs.'

They settled down to their game, and Adrian wandered about the room, endeavouring to still the riot of emotion which his recent interview with Sir Jasper Addleton had aroused in his bosom. All that remained for him to do now, he reflected, was by some means or other to remove the existing prejudice against him from Lord Brangbolton's mind.

It would not be easy, of course. To begin with, there was the matter of his straitened means.

He suddenly remembered that he had not yet looked at the cheque which the financier had handed him. He pulled it out of his pocket.

And, having glanced at it, Adrian Mulliner swayed like a poplar in a storm.

Just what he had expected, he could not have said. A fiver, possibly. At the most, a tenner. Just a trifling gift, he had imagined, with which to buy himself a cigarette-lighter, a fish-slice, or an egg-boiler.

The cheque was for a hundred thousand pounds.

So great was the shock that, as Adrian caught sight of himself in the mirror opposite to which he was standing, he scarcely recognized the face in the glass. He seemed to be seeing it through a mist. Then the mist cleared, and he saw not only his own face clearly, but also that of Lord Brangbolton, who was in the act of cutting against his left-hand neighbour, Lord Knubble of Knopp.

And, as he thought of the effect this sudden accession of wealth must surely have on the father of the girl he loved, there came into Adrian's face a sudden, swift smile.

And simultaneously from behind him he heard a gasping exclamation, and, looking in the mirror, he met Lord Brangbolton's eyes. Always a little prominent, they were now almost prawn-like in their convexity.

Lord Knubble of Knopp had produced a bank-note from his pocket and was pushing it along the table.

'Another ace!' he exclaimed. 'Well I'm dashed!'

Lord Brangbolton had risen from his chair.

'Excuse me,' he said in a strange, croaking voice. 'I just want to have a little chat with my friend, my dear old friend, Mulliner here. Might I have a word in private with you, Mr Mulliner?'

There was silence between the two men until they had reached a corner of the terrace out of earshot of the library window. Then Lord Brangbolton cleared his throat.

'Mulliner,' he began, 'or, rather – what is your Christian name?'

'Adrian.'

'Adrian, my dear fellow,' said Lord Brangbolton, 'my memory is not what it should be, but I seem to have a distinct recollection that, when I was in my bath before dinner, you said something about wanting to marry my daughter Millicent.'

'I did,' replied Adrian. 'And, if your objections to me as a suitor were mainly financial, let me assure you that, since we last spoke, I have become a wealthy man.'

'I never had any objections to you, Adrian, financial or otherwise,' said Lord Brangbolton, patting his arm affectionately. 'I have always felt that the man my daughter married ought to be a fine, warm-hearted young fellow like you. For you, Adrian,' he proceeded, 'are essentially warm-hearted. You would never dream of distressing a father-in-law by mentioning any . . . any little . . . well, in short, I saw from your smile in there that you had noticed that I was introducing into

27

that game of Blind Hooky — or, rather, Persian Monarchs — certain little — shall I say variations, designed to give it additional interest and excitement, and I feel sure that you would scorn to embarrass a father-in-law by . . . Well, to cut a long story short, my boy, take Millicent and with her a father's blessing.'

He extended his hand. Adrian clasped it warmly.

'I am the happiest man in the world,' he said, smiling.

Lord Brangbolton winced.

'Do you mind not doing that?' he said.

'I only smiled,' said Adrian.

'I know,' said Lord Brangbolton.

Little remains to be told. Adrian and Millicent were married three months later at a fashionable West End church. All Society was there. The presents were both numerous and costly, and the bride looked charming. The service was conducted by the Very Reverend the Dean of Bittlesham.

It was in the vestry afterwards, as Adrian looked at Millicent and seemed to realize for the first time that all his troubles were over and that this lovely girl was indeed his, for better or worse, that a full sense of his happiness swept over the young man.

All through the ceremony he had been grave, as befitted a man at the most serious point of his career. But now, fizzing as if with some spiritual yeast, he clasped her in his arms and over her shoulder his face broke into a quick smile.

He found himself looking into the eyes of the Dean of Bittlesham. A moment later he felt a tap on his arm.

'Might I have a word with you in private, Mr Mulliner?' said the Dean in a low voice.

Another day had dawned all hot and fresh and, in pursuance of my unswerving policy at that time, I was singing 'Sonny Boy' in my bath, when there was a soft step without and Jeeves's voice came filtering through the woodwork.

'I beg your pardon, sir.'

I had just got to that bit about the Angels being lonely, where you need every ounce of concentration in order to make the spectacular finish, but I signed off courteously.

'Yes, Jeeves? Say on.'

'Mr Glossop, sir.'

'What about him?'

'He is in the sitting-room, sir.'

'Young Tuppy Glossop?'

'Yes, sir.'

'In the sitting-room?'

'Yes, sir.'

'Desiring speech with me?'

'Yes, sir.'

'H'm!'

'Sir?'

'I only said H'm.'

And I'll tell you why I said H'm. It was because the man's story had interested me strangely. The news that Tuppy was visiting me at my flat, at an hour when he must have known that I would be in my bath and consequently in a strong strategic position to heave a wet sponge at him, surprised me considerably.

I hopped out with some briskness and, slipping a couple of towels about the limbs and torso, made for the sitting-room. I found young Tuppy at the piano, playing 'Sonny Boy' with one finger.

'What ho!' I said, not without a certain hauteur.

'Oh, hullo, Bertie,' said young Tuppy. 'I say, Bertie, I want to see you about something important.'

It seemed to me that the bloke was embarrassed. He had moved to the mantelpiece, and now he broke a vase in rather a constrained way.

'The fact is, Bertie, I'm engaged.'

'Engaged?'

'Engaged,' said young Tuppy, coyly dropping a photograph frame into the fender. 'Practically, that is.'

'Practically?'

'Yes. You'll like her, Bertie. Her name is Cora Bellinger. She's studying for Opera. Wonderful voice she has. Also dark, flashing eyes and a great soul.'

'How do you mean, practically?'

'Well, it's this way. Before ordering the trousseau, there is one little point she wants cleared up. You see, what with her great soul and all that, she has a rather serious outlook on life: and the one thing she absolutely bars is anything in the shape of hearty humour. You know, practical joking and so forth. She said if she thought I was a practical joker she would never speak to me again. And unfortunately she appears to have heard about that little affair at the Drones – I expect you have forgotten all about that, Bertie?'

'I have not!'

'No, no, not forgotten exactly. What I mean is, nobody laughs more heartily at the recollection than you. And what I want you to do, old man, is to seize an early opportunity of taking Cora aside and categorically denying that there is any truth in the story. My happiness, Bertie, is in your hands, if you know what I mean.'

Well, of course, if he put it like that, what could I do? We Woosters have our code.

'Oh, all right,' I said, but far from brightly.

'Splendid fellow!'

'When do I meet this blighted female?'

'Don't call her "this blighted female", Bertie, old man. I have planned all that out. I will bring her round here to-day for a spot of lunch.'

'What!'

'At one-thirty. Right. Good. Fine. Thanks. I knew I could rely on you.'

He pushed off, and I turned to Jeeves, who had shimmered in with the morning meal.

'Lunch for three to-day, Jeeves,' I said.

'Very good, sir.'

'You know, Jeeves, it's a bit thick. You remember my telling you about what Mr Glossop did to me that night at the Drones?'

'Yes, sir.'

'For months I have been cherishing dreams of getting a bit of my own back. And now, so far from crushing him into the dust, I've got to fill him and fiancée with rich food and generally rally round and be the good angel.'

'Life is like that, sir.'

'True, Jeeves. What have we here?' I asked, inspecting the tray.

'Kippered herrings, sir.'

'And I shouldn't wonder,' I said, for I was in thoughtful mood, 'if even herrings haven't troubles of their own.'

'Quite possibly, sir.'

'I mean, apart from getting kippered.'

'Yes, sir.'

'And so it goes on, Jeeves, so it goes on.'

I can't say I exactly saw eye to eye with young Tuppy in his admiration for the Bellinger female. Delivered on the mat at one-twenty-five, she proved to be an upstanding light-heavyweight of some thirty summers, with a commanding eye and a square chin which I, personally, would have steered clear of. She seemed to me a good deal like what Cleopatra would have been after going in too freely for the starches and cereals. I don't know why it is, but women who have anything to do with Opera, even if they're only studying for it, always appear to run to surplus poundage.

Tuppy, however, was obviously all for her. His whole demeanour, both before and during lunch, was that of one striving to be worthy of a noble soul. When Jeeves offered him a cocktail, he practically recoiled as from a serpent. It was terrible to see the change which love had effected in the man. The spectacle put me off my food.

At half-past two, the Bellinger left to go to a singing lesson. Tuppy trotted after her to the door, bleating and frisking a goodish bit, and then came back and looked at me in a goofy sort of way.

'Well, Bertie?'

'Well, what?'

'I mean, isn't she?'

'Oh, rather,' I said, humouring the poor fish.

'Wonderful eyes?'

'Oh, rather.'

'Wonderful figure?'

'Oh, quite.'

'Wonderful voice?'

Here I was able to intone the response with a little more heartiness. The Bellinger, at Tuppy's request, had sung us a few songs before digging in at the trough, and nobody could have denied that her pipes were in great shape. Plaster was still falling from the ceiling.

'Terrific,' I said.

Tuppy sighed, and, having helped himself to about four inches of whisky and one of soda, took a deep, refreshing draught.

'Ah!' he said. 'I needed that.'

'Why didn't you have it at lunch?'

'Well, it's this way,' said Tuppy. 'I have not actually ascertained what Cora's opinions are on the subject of the taking of slight snorts from time to time, but I thought it more prudent to lay off. The view I took was that laying off would seem to indicate the serious mind. It is touch-and-go, as you might say, at the moment, and the smallest thing may turn the scale.'

'What beats me is how on earth you expect to make her think you've got a mind at all – let alone a serious one.'

'I have my methods.'

'I bet they're rotten.'

'You do, do you?' said Tuppy warmly. 'Well, let me tell you, my lad, that that's exactly what they're anything but. I am handling this affair with consummate generalship. Do you remember Beefy Bingham who was at Oxford with us?'

'I ran into him only the other day. He's a parson now.'

'Yes. Down in the East End. Well, he runs a Lads' Club

for the local toughs – you know the sort of thing – cocoa and back-gammon in the reading-room and occasional clean, bright entertainments in the Oddfellows' Hall: and I've been helping him. I don't suppose I've passed an evening away from the back-gammon board for weeks. Cora is extremely pleased. I've got her to promise to sing on Tuesday at Beefy's next clean, bright entertainment.'

'You have?'

'I absolutely have. And now mark my devilish ingenuity, Bertie. I'm going to sing, too.'

'Why do you suppose that's going to get you anywhere?'

'Because the way I intend to sing the song I intend to sing will prove to her that there are great deeps in my nature, whose existence she has not suspected. She will see that rough, unlettered audience wiping the tears out of its bally eyes and she will say to herself "What ho! The old egg really has a soul!" For it is not one of your mouldy comic songs, Bertie. No low buffoonery of that sort for me. It is all about Angels being lonely and what not—'

I uttered a sharp cry.

'You don't mean you're going to sing "Sonny Boy"?'

'I jolly well do.'

I was shocked. Yes, dash it, I was shocked. You see, I held strong views on 'Sonny Boy'. I considered it a song only to be attempted by a few of the elect in the privacy of the bathroom. And the thought of it being murdered in open Oddfellows' Hall by a man who could treat a pal as young Tuppy had treated me that night at the Drones sickened me. Yes, sickened me.

I hadn't time, however, to express my horror and disgust, for at this juncture Jeeves came in.

'Mrs Travers has just rung up on the telephone, sir. She desired me to say that she will be calling to see you in a few minutes.'

'Contents noted, Jeeves,' I said. 'Now listen, Tuppy—'

I stopped. The fellow wasn't there.

'What have you done with him, Jeeves?' I asked.

'Mr Glossop has left, sir.'

'Left? How can he have left? He was sitting there—'

'That is the front door closing now, sir.'

'But what made him shoot off like that?'

'Possibly Mr Glossop did not wish to meet Mrs Travers, sir.'

'Why not?'

'I could not say, sir. But undoubtedly at the mention of Mrs Travers' name he rose very swiftly.'

'Strange, Jeeves.'

'Yes, sir.'

I turned to a subject of more moment.

'Jeeves,' I said, 'Mr Glossop proposes to sing "Sonny Boy" at an entertainment down in the East End next Tuesday.'

'Indeed, sir?'

'Before an audience consisting mainly of coster-mongers, with a sprinkling of whelk-stall owners, purveyors of blood-oranges, and minor pugilists.'

'Indeed, sir?'

'Make a note to remind me to be there. He will infallibly get the bird, and I want to witness his downfall.'

'Very good, sir.'

'And when Mrs Travers arrives, I shall be in the sitting-room.'

Those who know Bertram Wooster best are aware that in his journey through life he is impeded and generally snootered by about as scaly a platoon of aunts as was ever assembled. But there is one exception to the general ghastliness – viz., my Aunt Dahlia. She married old Tom Travers the year Bluebottle won the Cambridgeshire, and is one of the best. It is always a pleasure to me to chat with her, and it was with a courtly geniality that I rose to receive her as she sailed over the threshold at about two-fifty-five.

She seemed somewhat perturbed, and snapped into the agenda without delay. Aunt Dahlia is one of those big, hearty women. She used to go in a lot for hunting, and she generally speaks as if she had just sighted a fox on a hillside half a mile away.

'Bertie,' she cried, in the manner of one encouraging a bevy of hounds to renewed efforts. 'I want your help.'

'And you shall have it, Aunt Dahlia,' I replied suavely. 'I can honestly say that there is no one to whom I would more readily do a good turn than yourself; no one to whom I am more delighted to be—'

'Less of it,' she begged, 'less of it. You know that friend of yours, young Glossop?'

'He's just been lunching here.'

'He has, has he? Well, I wish you'd poisoned his soup.'

'We didn't have soup. And, when you describe him as a friend of mine, I wouldn't quite say the term absolutely squared with the facts. Some time ago, one night when we had been dining together at the Drones——'

At this point Aunt Dahlia — a little brusquely, it seemed to me — said that she would rather wait for the story of my life till she could get it in book-form. I could see now that she was definitely not her usual sunny self, so I shelved my personal grievances and asked what was biting her.

'It's that young hound Glossop,' she said.

'What's he been doing?'

'Breaking Angela's heart.' (Angela. Daughter of above. My cousin. Quite a good egg.)

'Breaking Angela's heart?'

'Yes . . . Breaking . . . Angela's . . . HEART!'

'You say he's breaking Angela's heart?'

She begged me in rather a feverish way to suspend the vaudeville cross-talk stuff.

'How's he doing that?' I asked.

'With his neglect. With his low, callous, double-crossing duplicity.'

'Duplicity is the word, Aunt Dahlia,' I said. 'In treating of young Tuppy Glossop, it springs naturally

to the lips. Let me just tell you what he did to me one
night at the Drones. We had finished dinner—'

'Ever since the beginning of the season, up till about
three weeks ago, he was all over Angela. The sort of
thing which, when I was a girl, we should have described
as courting—'

'Or wooing?'

'Wooing or courting, whichever you like.'

'Whichever *you* like, Aunt Dahlia,' I said courteously.

'Well, anyway, he haunted the house, lapped up
daily lunches, danced with her half the night, and so
on, till naturally the poor kid, who's quite off her oats
about him, took it for granted that it was only a question of time before he suggested that they should feed
for life out of the same crib. And now he's gone and
dropped her like a hot brick, and I hear he's infatuated
with some girl he met at a Chelsea tea-party – a girl
named – now, what was it?'

'Cora Bellinger.'

'How do you know?'

'She was lunching here to-day.'

'He brought her?'

'Yes.'

'What's she like?'

'Pretty massive. In shape, a bit on the lines of the
Albert Hall.'

'Did he seem very fond of her?'

'Couldn't take his eyes off the chassis.'

'The modern young man,' said Aunt Dahlia, 'is a

congenital idiot and wants a nurse to lead him by the hand and some strong attendant to kick him regularly at intervals of a quarter of an hour.'

I tried to point out the silver lining.

'If you ask me, Aunt Dahlia,' I said, 'I think Angela is well out of it. This Glossop is a tough baby. One of London's toughest. I was trying to tell you just now what he did to me one night at the Drones. First having got me in sporting mood with a bottle of the ripest, he betted I wouldn't swing myself across the swimming-bath by the ropes and rings. I knew I could do it on my head, so I took him on, exulting in the fun, so to speak. And when I'd done half the trip and was going as strong as dammit, I found he had looped the last rope back against the rail, leaving me no alternative but to drop into the depths and swim ashore in correct evening costume.'

'He did?'

'He certainly did. It was months ago, and I haven't got really dry yet. You wouldn't want your daughter to marry a man capable of a thing like that?'

'On the contrary, you restore my faith in the young hound. I see that there must be lots of good in him, after all. And I want this Bellinger business broken up, Bertie.'

'How?'

'I don't care how. Any way you please.'

'But what can I do?'

'Do? Why, put the whole thing before your man

Jeeves. Jeeves will find a way. One of the most capable fellers I ever met. Put the thing squarely up to Jeeves and tell him to let his mind play round the topic.'

'There may be something in what you say, Aunt Dahlia,' I said thoughtfully.

'Of course there is,' said Aunt Dahlia. 'A little thing like this will be child's play to Jeeves. Get him working on it, and I'll look in to-morrow to hear the result.'

With which, she biffed off, and I summoned Jeeves to the presence.

'Jeeves,' I said, 'you have heard all?'

'Yes, sir.'

'I thought you would. My Aunt Dahlia has what you might call a carrying voice. Has it ever occurred to you that, if all other sources of income failed, she could make a good living calling the cattle home across the Sands of Dee?'

'I had not considered the point, sir, but no doubt you are right.'

'Well, how do we go? What is your reaction? I think we should do our best to help and assist.'

'Yes, sir.'

'I am fond of my Aunt Dahlia and I am fond of my cousin Angela. Fond of them both, if you get my drift. What the misguided girl finds to attract her in young Tuppy, I cannot say, Jeeves, and you cannot say. But apparently she loves the man – which shows it can be done, a thing I wouldn't have believed myself – and is pining away like—'

'Patience on a monument, sir.'

'Like Patience, as you very shrewdly remark, on a monument. So we must cluster round. Bend your brain to the problem, Jeeves. It is one that will tax you to the uttermost.'

Aunt Dahlia blew in on the morrow, and I rang the bell for Jeeves. He appeared looking brainier than one could have believed possible – sheer intellect shining from every feature – and I could see at once that the engine had been turning over.

'Speak, Jeeves,' I said.

'Very good, sir.'

'You have brooded?'

'Yes, sir.'

'With what success?'

'I have a plan, sir, which I fancy may produce satisfactory results.'

'Let's have it,' said Aunt Dahlia.

'In affairs of this description, madam, the first essential is to study the psychology of the individual.'

'The what of the individual?'

'The psychology, madam.'

'He means the psychology,' I said. 'And by psychology, Jeeves, you imply——?'

'The natures and dispositions of the principals in the matter, sir.'

'You mean, what they're like?'

'Precisely, sir.'

'Does he talk like this to you when you're alone, Bertie?' asked Aunt Dahlia.

'Sometimes. Occasionally. And, on the other hand, sometimes not. Proceed, Jeeves.'

'Well, sir, if I may say so, the thing that struck me most forcibly about Miss Bellinger when she was under my observation was that hers was a somewhat hard and intolerant nature. I could envisage Miss Bellinger applauding success. I could not so easily see her pitying and sympathizing with failure. Possibly you will recall, sir, her attitude when Mr Glossop endeavoured to light her cigarette with his automatic lighter? I thought I detected a certain impatience at his inability to produce the necessary flame.'

'True, Jeeves. She ticked him off.'

'Precisely, sir.'

'Let me get this straight,' said Aunt Dahlia, looking a bit fogged. 'You think that, if he goes on trying to light her cigarettes with his automatic lighter long enough, she will eventually get fed up and hand him the mitten? Is that the idea?'

'I merely mentioned the episode, madam, as an indication of Miss Bellinger's somewhat ruthless nature.'

'Ruthless,' I said, 'is right. The Bellinger is hard-boiled. Those eyes. That chin. I could read them. A woman of blood and iron, if ever there was one.'

'Precisely, sir. I think, therefore, that, should Miss Bellinger be a witness of Mr Glossop appearing to disadvantage in public, she would cease to entertain affection for him. In the event, for instance, of his failing to please the audience on Tuesday with his singing—'

I saw daylight.

'By Jove, Jeeves! You mean if he gets the bird, all will be off?'

'I shall be greatly surprised if such is not the case, sir.'

I shook my head.

'We cannot leave this thing to chance, Jeeves. Young Tuppy, singing "Sonny Boy", is the likeliest prospect for the bird that I can think of – but, no – you must see for yourself that we can't simply trust to luck.'

'We need not trust to luck, sir. I would suggest that you approach your friend, Mr Bingham, and volunteer your services as a performer at his forthcoming entertainment. It could readily be arranged that you sang immediately before Mr Glossop. I fancy, sir, that, if Mr Glossop were to sing "Sonny Boy" directly after you, too, had sung "Sonny Boy", the audience would respond satisfactorily. By the time Mr Glossop began to sing, they would have lost their taste for that particular song and would express their feelings warmly.'

'Jeeves,' said Aunt Dahlia, 'you're a marvel!'

'Thank you, madam.'

'Jeeves,' I said, 'you're an ass!'

'What do you mean, he's an ass?' said Aunt Dahlia hotly. 'I think it's the greatest scheme I ever heard.'

'Me sing "Sonny Boy" at Beefy Bingham's clean, bright entertainment? I can see myself!'

'You sing it daily in your bath, sir. Mr Wooster,' said Jeeves, turning to Aunt Dahlia, 'has a pleasant, light baritone——'

'I bet he has,' said Aunt Dahlia.

I froze the man with a look.

'Between singing "Sonny Boy" in one's bath, Jeeves, and singing it before a hall full of assorted blood-orange merchants and their young, there is a substantial difference.'

'Bertie,' said Aunt Dahlia, 'you'll sing, and like it!'

'I will not.'

'Bertie!'

'Nothing will induce——'

'Bertie,' said Aunt Dahlia firmly, 'you will sing "Sonny Boy" on Tuesday, the third *prox.*, and sing it like a lark at sunrise, or may an aunt's curse——'

'I won't!'

'Think of Angela!'

'Dash Angela!'

'Bertie!'

'No, I mean, hang it all!'

'You won't?'

'No, I won't.'

'That is your last word, is it?'

'It is. Once and for all, Aunt Dahlia, nothing will induce me to let out so much as a single note.'

And so that afternoon I sent a pre-paid wire to Beefy Bingham, offering my services in the cause, and by nightfall the thing was fixed up. I was billed to perform next but one after the intermission. Following me, came Tuppy. And, immediately after him, Miss Cora Bellinger, the well-known operatic soprano.

'Jeeves,' I said that evening – and I said it coldly – 'I shall be obliged if you will pop round to the nearest music-shop and procure me a copy of "Sonny Boy". It will now be necessary for me to learn both verse and refrain. Of the trouble and nervous strain which this will involve, I say nothing.'

'Very good, sir.'

'But this I do say—'

'I had better be starting immediately, sir, or the shop will be closed.'

'Ha!' I said.

And I meant it to sting.

Although I had steeled myself to the ordeal before me and had set out full of the calm, quiet courage which makes men do desperate deeds with careless smiles, I must admit that there was a moment, just after I had entered the Oddfellows' Hall at Bermondsey East and run an eye over the assembled pleasure-seekers, when it needed all the bull-dog pluck of the Woosters to keep me from calling it a day and taking a cab back to civilization. The clean, bright entertainment was in full swing when I arrived, and somebody who looked as if he might be the local undertaker was reciting 'Gunga Din'. And the audience, though not actually chi-yiking in the full technical sense of the term, had a grim look which I didn't like at all. The mere sight of them gave me the sort of feeling Shadrach, Meshach and Abednego must have had when preparing to enter the burning, fiery furnace.

Scanning the multitude, it seemed to me that they were for the nonce suspending judgement. Did you ever tap on the door of one of those New York speakeasy places and see the grille snap back and a Face appear? There is one long, silent moment when its eyes are fixed on yours and all your past life seems to rise up before you. Then you say that you are a friend of Mr Zinzinheimer and he told you they would treat you right if you mentioned his name, and the strain relaxes. Well, these costermongers and whelk-stallers appeared to me to be looking just like that Face. Start something, they seemed to say, and they would know what to do about it. And I couldn't help feeling that my singing 'Sonny Boy' would come, in their opinion, under the head of starting something.

'A nice, full house, sir,' said a voice at my elbow. It was Jeeves, watching the proceedings with an indulgent eye.

'You here, Jeeves?' I said, coldly.

'Yes, sir. I have been present since the commencement.'

'Oh?' I said. 'Any casualties yet?'

'Sir?'

'You know what I mean, Jeeves,' I said sternly, 'and don't pretend you don't. Anybody got the bird yet?'

'Oh, no, sir.'

'I shall be the first, you think?'

'No, sir. I see no reason to expect such a misfortune. I anticipate that you will be well received.'

A sudden thought struck me.

'And you think everything will go according to plan?'

'Yes, sir.'

'Well, I don't,' I said. 'And I'll tell you why I don't. I've spotted a flaw in your beastly scheme.'

'A flaw, sir?'

'Yes. Do you suppose for a moment that, if when Mr Glossop hears me singing that dashed song, he'll come calmly on a minute after me and sing it too? Use your intelligence, Jeeves. He will perceive the chasm in his path and pause in time. He will back out and refuse to go on at all.'

'Mr Glossop will not hear you sing, sir. At my advice, he has stepped across the road to the Jug and Bottle, an establishment immediately opposite the hall, and he intends to remain there until it is time for him to appear on the platform.'

'Oh?' I said.

'If I might suggest it, sir, there is another house named the Goat and Grapes only a short distance down the street. I think it might be a judicious move——'

'If I were to put a bit of custom in their way?'

'It would ease the nervous strain of waiting, sir.'

I had not been feeling any too pleased with the man

for having let me in for this ghastly binge, but at these words, I'm bound to say, my austerity softened a trifle. He was undoubtedly right. He had studied the psychology of the individual, and it had not led him astray. A quiet ten minutes at the Goat and Grapes was exactly what my system required. To buzz off there and inhale a couple of swift whisky-and-sodas was with Bertram Wooster the work of a moment.

The treatment worked like magic. What they had put into the stuff, besides vitriol, I could not have said; but it completely altered my outlook on life. That curious, gulpy feeling passed. I was no longer conscious of the sagging sensation at the knees. The limbs ceased to quiver gently, the tongue became loosened in its socket, and the backbone stiffened. Pausing merely to order and swallow another of the same, I bade the barmaid a cheery good night, nodded affably to one or two fellows in the bar whose faces I liked, and came prancing back to the hall, ready for anything.

And shortly afterwards I was on the platform with about a million bulging eyes goggling up at me. There was a rummy sort of buzzing in my ears, and then through the buzzing I heard the sound of a piano starting to tinkle: and, commending my soul to God, I took a good, long breath and charged in.

Well, it was a close thing. The whole incident is a bit blurred, but I seem to recollect a kind of murmur as I hit the refrain. I thought at the time it was an attempt on the part of the many-headed to join in the chorus, and at the moment it rather encouraged me. I passed the thing over the larynx with all the vim at my disposal, hit the high note, and off gracefully into the wings. I didn't come on again to take a bow. I just receded and oiled round to where Jeeves awaited me among the standees at the back.

'Well, Jeeves,' I said, anchoring myself at his side and brushing the honest sweat from the brow, 'they didn't rush the platform.'

'No, sir.'

'But you can spread it about that that's the last time I perform outside my bath. My swan-song, Jeeves. Anybody who wants to hear me in future must present himself at the bathroom door and shove his ear against the keyhole. I may be wrong, but it seemed to me that towards the end they were hotting up a trifle. The bird was hovering in the air. I could hear the beating of its wings.'

'I did detect a certain restlessness, sir, in the audience. I fancy they had lost their taste for that particular melody.'

'Eh?'

'I should have informed you earlier, sir, that the song had already been sung twice before you arrived.'

'What!'

'Yes, sir. Once by a lady and once by a gentleman. It is a very popular song, sir.'

I gaped at the man. That, with this knowledge, he

could calmly have allowed the young master to step straight into the jaws of death, so to speak, paralysed me. It seemed to show that the old feudal spirit had passed away altogether. I was about to give him my views on the matter in no uncertain fashion, when I was stopped by the spectacle of young Tuppy lurching on to the platform.

Young Tuppy had the unmistakable air of a man who has recently been round to the Jug and Bottle. A few cheery cries of welcome, presumably from some of his backgammon-playing pals who felt that blood was thicker than water, had the effect of causing the genial smile on his face to widen till it nearly met at the back. He was plainly feeling about as good as a man can feel and still remain on his feet. He waved a kindly hand to his supporters, and bowed in a regal sort of manner, rather like an Eastern monarch acknowledging the plaudits of the mob.

Then the female at the piano struck up the opening bars of 'Sonny Boy', and Tuppy swelled like a balloon, clasped his hands together, rolled his eyes up at the ceiling in a manner denoting Soul, and began.

I think the populace was too stunned for the moment to take immediate steps. It may seem incredible, but I give you my word that young Tuppy got right through the verse without so much as a murmur. Then they all seemed to pull themselves together.

A costermonger, roused, is a terrible thing. I had never

seen the proletariat really stirred before, and I'm bound to say it rather awed me. I mean, it gave you some idea of what it must have been like during the French Revolution. From every corner of the hall there proceeded simultaneously the sort of noise which you hear, they tell me, at one of those East End boxing places when the referee disqualifies the popular favourite and makes the quick dash for life. And then they passed beyond mere words and began to introduce the vegetable motive.

I don't know why, but somehow I had got it into my head that the first thing thrown at Tuppy would be a potato. One gets these fancies. It was, however, as a matter of fact, a banana, and I saw in an instant that the choice had been made by wiser heads than mine. These blokes who have grown up from childhood in the knowledge of how to treat a dramatic entertainment that doesn't please them are aware by a sort of instinct just what to do for the best, and the moment I saw that banana splash on Tuppy's shirt-front I realized how infinitely more effective and artistic it was than any potato could have been.

Not that the potato school of thought had not also its supporters. As the proceedings warmed up, I noticed several intelligent-looking fellows who threw nothing else.

The effect on young Tuppy was rather remarkable. His eyes bulged and his hair seemed to stand up, and yet his mouth went on opening and shutting, and you could see that in a dazed, automatic way he was still singing 'Sonny Boy'. Then, coming out of his trance, he began to pull for the shore with some rapidity. The last seen of him, he was beating a tomato to the exit by a short head.

Presently the tumult and the shouting died. I turned to Jeeves.

'Painful, Jeeves,' I said. 'But what would you?'

'Yes, sir.'

'The surgeon's knife, what?'

'Precisely, sir.'

'Well, with this happening beneath her eyes, I think we may definitely consider the Glossop–Bellinger romance off.'

'Yes, sir.'

At this point old Beefy Bingham came out on to the platform.

'Ladies and gentlemen,' said old Beefy.

I supposed that he was about to rebuke his flock for the recent expression of feeling. But such was not the case. No doubt he was accustomed by now to the whole-some give-and-take of these clean, bright entertainments and had ceased to think it worth while to make any comment when there was a certain liveliness.

'Ladies and gentlemen,' said old Beefy, 'the next item on the programme was to have been Songs by Miss Cora Bellinger, the well-known operatic soprano. I have just received a telephone-message from Miss Bellinger, saying that her car has broken down. She is, however, on her way here in a cab and will arrive shortly. Meanwhile, our friend Mr Enoch Simpson will recite "Dangerous Dan McGrew".'

I clutched at Jeeves.

'Jeeves! You heard?'

'Yes, sir.'

'She wasn't there!'

'No, sir.'

'She saw nothing of Tuppy's Waterloo.'

'No, sir.'

'The whole bally scheme has blown a fuse.'

'Yes, sir.'

'Come, Jeeves,' I said, and those standing by wondered, no doubt, what had caused that clean-cut face to grow so pale and set. 'I have been subjected to a nervous strain unparalleled since the days of the early Martyrs. I have lost pounds in weight and permanently injured my entire system. I have gone through an ordeal, the recollection of which will make me wake up screaming in the night for months to come. And all for nothing. Let us go.'

'If you have no objection, sir, I would like to witness the remainder of the entertainment.'

'Suit yourself, Jeeves,' I said moodily. 'Personally, my heart is dead and I am going to look in at the Goat and Grapes for another of their cyanide specials and then home.'

It must have been about half-past ten, and I was in the old sitting-room sombrely sucking down a more or less final restorative, when the front-door bell rang, and there on the mat was young Tuppy. He looked like a man who has passed through some great experience and stood face to face with his soul. He had the beginnings of a black eye.

'Oh, hullo, Bertie,' said young Tuppy.

He came in, and hovered about the mantelpiece as if he were looking for things to fiddle with and break.

'I've just been singing at Beefy Bingham's entertainment,' he said after a pause.

'Oh?' I said. 'How did you go?'

'Like a breeze,' said young Tuppy. 'Held them spellbound.'

'Knocked 'em, eh?'

'Cold,' said young Tuppy. 'Not a dry eye.'

And this, mark you, a man who had had a good upbringing and had, no doubt, spent years at his mother's knee being taught to tell the truth.

'I suppose Miss Bellinger is pleased?'

'Oh, yes. Delighted.'

'So now everything's all right?'

'Oh, quite.'

Tuppy paused.

'On the other hand, Bertie—'

'Yes?'

'Well, I've been thinking things over. Somehow I don't believe Miss Bellinger is the mate for me, after all.'

'You don't?'

'No, I don't.'

'Why don't you?'

'Oh, I don't know. These things sort of flash on you. I respect Miss Bellinger, Bertie. I admire her. But — er — well, I can't help feeling now that a sweet, gentle girl — er — like your cousin Angela, for instance, Bertie, would — er — in fact— well, what I came round for was to ask if you would 'phone Angela and find out how she reacts to the idea of coming out with me to-night to the Berkeley for a segment of supper and a spot of dancing.'

'Go ahead. There's the 'phone.'

'No, I'd rather you asked her, Bertie. What with one thing and another, if you paved the way— You see, there's just a chance that she may be— I mean, you know how misunderstandings occur— and— well, what I'm driving at, Bertie, old man, is that I'd rather you surged round and did a bit of paving, if you don't mind.'

I went to the 'phone and called up Aunt Dahlia's.

'She says come right along,' I said.

'Tell her,' said Tuppy in a devout sort of voice, 'that I will be with her in something under a couple of ticks.'

He had barely biffed, when I heard a click in the key-hole and a soft padding in the passage without.

'Jeeves,' I called.

'Sir?' said Jeeves, manifesting himself.

'Jeeves, a remarkably rummy thing has happened. Mr Glossop has just been here. He tells me that it is all off between him and Miss Bellinger.'

'Yes, sir.'

'You don't seem surprised.'

'No, sir. I confess I had anticipated some such eventuality.'

'Eh? What gave you that idea?'

'It came to me, sir, when I observed Miss Bellinger strike Mr Glossop in the eye.'

'Strike him!'

'Yes, sir.'

'In the eye?'

'The right eye, sir.'

I clutched the brow.

'What on earth made her do that?'

'I fancy she was a little upset, sir, at the reception accorded to her singing.'

'Great Scott! Don't tell me she got the bird, too?'

'Yes, sir.'

'But why? She's got a red-hot voice.'

'Yes, sir. But I think the audience resented her choice of a song.'

'Jeeves!' Reason was beginning to do a bit of tottering on its throne. 'You aren't going to stand there and tell me that Miss Bellinger sang "Sonny Boy", too!'

'Yes, sir. And – rashly, in my opinion – brought a large doll on to the platform to sing it to. The audience affected to mistake it for a ventriloquist's dummy, and there was some little disturbance.'

'But, Jeeves, what a coincidence!'

'Not altogether, sir. I ventured to take the liberty of

accosting Miss Bellinger on her arrival at the hall and recalling myself to her recollection. I then said that Mr Glossop had asked me to request her that as a particular favour to him – the song being a favourite of his – she would sing "Sonny Boy". And when she found that you and Mr Glossop had also sung the song immediately before her, I rather fancy that she supposed that she had been made the victim of a practical pleasantry by Mr Glossop. Will there be anything further, sir?'

'No, thanks.'

'Good night, sir.'

'Good night, Jeeves,' I said reverently.

# THE GREAT SERMON HANDICAP

After Goodwood's over, I generally find that I get a bit restless. I'm not much of a lad for the birds and the trees and the great open spaces as a rule, but there's no doubt that London's not at its best in August, and rather tends to give me the pip and make me think of popping down into the country till things have bucked up a trifle. London, about a couple of weeks after that spectacular finish of young Bingo's which I've just been telling you about, was empty and smelled of burning asphalt. All my pals were away, most of the theatres were shut, and they were taking up Piccadilly in large spadefuls.

It was most infernally hot. As I sat in the old flat one night trying to muster up energy enough to go to bed, I felt I couldn't stand it much longer: and when Jeeves came in with the tissue-restorers on a tray I put the thing to him squarely.

'Jeeves,' I said, wiping the brow and gasping like a stranded goldfish, 'it's beastly hot.'

'The weather *is* oppressive, sir.'

'Not all the soda, Jeeves.'

'No, sir.'

'I think we've had about enough of the metrop. for the time being, and require a change. Shift-ho, I think, Jeeves, what?'

'Just as you say, sir. There is a letter on the tray, sir.'

'By Jove, Jeeves, that was practically poetry. Rhymed, did you notice?' I opened the letter. 'I say, this is rather extraordinary.'

'Sir?'

'You know Twing Hall?'

'Yes, sir.'

'Well, Mr Little is there.'

'Indeed, sir?'

'Absolutely in the flesh. He's had to take another of those tutoring jobs.'

After that fearful mix-up at Goodwood, when young Bingo Little, a broken man, had touched me for a tenner and whizzed silently off into the unknown, I had been all over the place, asking mutual friends if they had heard anything of him, but nobody had. And all the time he had been at Twing Hall. Rummy. And I'll tell you why it was rummy. Twing Hall belongs to old Lord Wickhammersley, a great pal of my guv'nor's when he was alive, and I have a standing invitation to pop down there when I like. I generally put in a week or two some time in the summer, and I was thinking of going there before I read the letter.

'And, what's more, Jeeves, my cousin Claude, and my cousin Eustace — you remember them?'

'Very vividly, sir.'

'Well, they're down there, too, reading for some exam. or other with the vicar. I used to read with him myself at one time. He's known far and wide as a pretty hot coach for those of fairly feeble intellect. Well, when I tell you he got *me* through Smalls, you'll gather that he's a bit of a hummer. I call this most extraordinary.'

I read the letter again. It was from Eustace. Claude and Eustace are twins, and more or less generally admitted to be the curse of the human race.

> The Vicarage,
>
> Twing, Glos.
>
> DEAR BERTIE — Do you want to make a bit of money? I hear you had a bad Goodwood, so you probably do. Well, come down here quick and get in on the biggest sporting event of the season. I'll explain when I see you, but you can take it from me it's all right.
>
> Claude and I are with a reading-party at old Heppenstall's. There are nine of us, not counting your pal Bingo Little, who is tutoring the kid up at the Hall.
>
> Don't miss this golden opportunity, which may never occur again. Come and join us.
>
> Yours,
>
> Eustace.

I handed this to Jeeves. He studied it thoughtfully.

'What do you make of it? A rummy communication, what?'

'Very high-spirited young gentlemen, sir, Mr Claude and Mr Eustace. Up to some game, I should be disposed to imagine.'

'Yes. But what game, do you think?'

'It is impossible to say, sir. Did you observe that the letter continues over the page?'

'Eh, what?' I grabbed the thing. This was what was on the other side of the last page:

### SERMON HANDICAP
### RUNNERS AND BETTING
### PROBABLE STARTERS

Rev. Joseph Tucker (Badgwick), scratch.

Rev. Leonard Starkie (Stapleton), scratch.

Rev. Alexander Jones (Upper Bingley), receives three minutes.

Rev. W. Dix (Little Clickton-in-the-Wold), receives five minutes.

Rev. Francis Heppenstall (Twing), receives eight minutes.

Rev. Cuthbert Dibble (Boustead Parva), receives nine minutes.

Rev. Orlo Hough (Boustead Magna), receives nine minutes.

Rev. J. J. Roberts (Fale-by-the-Water), receives ten minutes.

Rev. G. Hayward (Lower Bingley), receives twelve minutes.

Rev. James Bates (Gandle-by-the-Hill), receives fifteen minutes.

(*The above have arrived.*)

Prices. — 5-2, Tucker, Starkie; 3-1, Jones; 9-2, Dix; 6-1, Heppenstall, Dibble, Hough; 100-8 any other.

It baffled me.

'Do you understand it, Jeeves?'

'No, sir.'

'Well, I think we ought to have a look into it, anyway, what?'

'Undoubtedly, sir.'

'Right-oh, then. Pack our spare dickey and a toothbrush in a neat brown-paper parcel, send a wire to Lord Wickhammersley to say we're coming, and buy two tickets on the five-ten at Paddington tomorrow.'

The five-ten was late as usual, and everybody was dressing for dinner when I arrived at the Hall. It was only by getting into my evening things in record time and taking the stairs to the dining-room in a couple of bounds that I managed to dead-heat with the soup. I slid into the vacant chair, and found that I was sitting next to old Wickhammersley's youngest daughter, Cynthia.

'Oh, hallo, old thing,' I said.

Great pals we've always been. In fact, there was a time when I had an idea I was in love with Cynthia. However, it blew over. A dashed pretty and lively and attractive girl, mind you, but full of ideals and all that. I may be wronging her, but I have an idea that she's the sort of girl who would want a fellow to carve out a career and what not. I know I've heard her speak favourably of Napoleon. So what with one thing and another the jolly old frenzy sort of petered out, and now we're just pals. I think she's a topper, and she thinks me next door to a looney, so everything's nice and matey.

'Well, Bertie, so you've arrived?'

'Oh, yes, I've arrived. Yes, here I am. I say, I seem to have plunged into the middle of quite a young dinner-party. Who are all these coves?'

'Oh, just people from round about. You know most of them. You remember Colonel Willis, and the Spencers—'

'Of course, yes. And there's old Heppenstall. Who's the other clergyman next to Mrs Spencer?'

'Mr Hayward, from Lower Bingley.'

'What an amazing lot of clergymen there are round here. Why, there's another, next to Mrs Willis.'

'That's Mr Bates, Mr Heppenstall's nephew. He's an assistant-master at Eton. He's down here during the summer holidays, acting as locum tenens for Mr Spettigue, the rector of Gandle-by-the-Hill.'

'I thought I knew his face. He was in his fourth year

at Oxford when I was a fresher. Rather a blood. Got his rowing-blue and all that.' I took another look round the table, and spotted young Bingo. 'Ah, there he is,' I said. 'There's the old egg.'

'There's who?'

'Young Bingo Little. Great pal of mine. He's tutoring your brother, you know.'

'Good gracious! Is he a friend of yours?'

'Rather! Known him all my life.'

'Then tell me, Bertie, is he at all weak in the head?'

'Weak in the head?'

'I don't mean simply because he's a friend of yours. But he's so strange in his manner.'

'How do you mean?'

'Well, he keeps looking at me so oddly.'

'Oddly? How? Give me an imitation.'

'I can't in front of all these people.'

'Yes, you can. I'll hold my napkin up.'

'All right, then. Quick. There!'

Considering that she had only about a second and a half to do it in, I must say it was a jolly fine exhibition. She opened her mouth and eyes pretty wide and let her jaw drop sideways, and managed to look so like a dyspeptic calf that I recognized the symptoms immediately.

'Oh, that's all right,' I said. 'No need to be alarmed. He's simply in love with you.'

'In love with me. Don't be absurd.'

'My dear old thing, you don't know young Bingo. He can fall in love with *anybody*.'

'Thank you!'

'Oh, I didn't mean it that way, you know. I don't wonder at his taking to you. Why, I was in love with you myself once.'

'Once? Ah! And all that remains now are the cold ashes? This isn't one of your tactful evenings, Bertie.'

'Well, my dear sweet thing, dash it all, considering that you gave me the bird and nearly laughed yourself into a permanent state of hiccoughs when I asked you—'

'Oh, I'm not reproaching you. No doubt there were faults on both sides. He's very good-looking, isn't he?'

'Good-looking? Bingo? Bingo good-looking? No, I say, come now, really!'

'I mean, compared with some people,' said Cynthia.

Some time after this, Lady Wickhammersley gave the signal for the females of the species to leg it, and they duly stampeded. I didn't get a chance of talking to young Bingo when they'd gone, and later, in the drawing-room, he didn't show up. I found him eventually in his room, lying on the bed with his feet on the rail, smoking a toofah. There was a note-book on the counterpane beside him.

'Hallo, old scream,' I said.

'Hallo, Bertie,' he replied, in what seemed to me rather a moody, distrait sort of manner.

'Rummy finding you down here. I take it your uncle cut off your allowance after that Goodwood binge and you had to take this tutoring job to keep the wolf from the door?'

'Correct,' said young Bingo tersely.

'Well, you might have let your pals know where you were.'

He frowned darkly.

'I didn't want them to know where I was. I wanted to creep away and hide myself. I've been through a bad time, Bertie, these last weeks. The sun ceased to shine—'

'That's curious. We've had gorgeous weather in London.'

'The birds ceased to sing—'

'What birds?'

'What the devil does it matter what birds?' said young Bingo, with some asperity. 'Any birds. The birds round about here. You don't expect me to specify them by their pet names, do you? I tell you, Bertie, it hit me hard at first, very hard.'

'What hit you?' I simply couldn't follow the blighter.

'Charlotte's calculated callousness.'

'Oh, ah!' I've seen poor old Bingo through so many unsuccessful love-affairs that I'd almost forgotten there was a girl mixed up with that Goodwood business. Of course! Charlotte Corday Rowbotham. And she had given him the raspberry, I remembered, and gone off with Comrade Butt.

'I went through torments. Recently, however, I've — er — bucked up a bit. Tell me, Bertie, what are you doing down here? I didn't know you knew these people.'

'Me? Why, I've known them since I was a kid.'

Young Bingo put his feet down with a thud.

'Do you mean to say you've known Lady Cynthia all that time?'

'Rather! She can't have been seven when I met her first.'

'Good Lord!' said young Bingo. He looked at me for the first time as though I amounted to something, and swallowed a mouthful of smoke the wrong way. 'I love that girl, Bertie,' he went on, when he'd finished coughing.

'Yes. Nice girl, of course.'

He eyed me with pretty deep loathing.

'Don't speak of her in that horrible casual way. She's an angel. An angel! Was she talking about me at all at dinner, Bertie?'

'Oh, yes.'

'What did she say?'

'I remember one thing. She said she thought you good-looking.'

Young Bingo closed his eyes in a sort of ecstasy. Then he picked up the note-book.

'Pop off now, old man, there's a good chap,' he said, in a hushed, far-away voice. 'I've got a bit of writing to do.'

'Writing?'

'Poetry, if you must know. I wish the dickens,' said young Bingo, not without some bitterness, 'she had been christened something except Cynthia. There isn't a dam' word in the language it rhymes with. Ye gods, how I could have spread myself if she had only been called Jane!'

Bright and early next morning, as I lay in bed blinking at the sunlight on the dressing-table and wondering when Jeeves was going to show up with a cup of tea, a heavy weight descended on my toes, and the voice of young Bingo polluted the air. The blighter had apparently risen with the lark.

'Leave me,' I said, 'I would be alone. I can't see anybody till I've had my tea.'

'When Cynthia smiles,' said young Bingo, 'the skies are blue; the world takes on a roseate hue; birds in the garden trill and sing, and Joy is king of everything, when Cynthia smiles.' He coughed, changing gears. 'When Cynthia frowns—'

'What the devil are you talking about?'

'I'm reading you my poem. The one I wrote to Cynthia last night. I'll go on, shall I?'

'No!'

'No?'

'No. I haven't had my tea.'

At this moment Jeeves came in with the good old beverage, and I sprang on it with a glad cry. After a couple of sips things looked a bit brighter. Even young Bingo didn't offend the eye to quite such an extent. By the time I'd finished the first cup I was a new man, so much so that I not only permitted but encouraged the poor fish to read the rest of the bally thing, and even went so far as to criticize the scansion of the fourth line of the fifth verse. We were still arguing the point when the door burst open and in blew Claude and Eustace. One of the things which discourages me about rural life is the frightful earliness with which events begin to break loose. I've stayed at places in the country where they've jerked me out of the dreamless at about six-thirty to go for a jolly swim in the lake. At Twing, thank heaven, they know me, and let me breakfast in bed.

The twins seemed pleased to see me.

'Good old Bertie!' said Claude.

'Stout fellow!' said Eustace. 'The Rev. told us you had arrived. I thought that letter of mine would fetch you.'

'You can always bank on Bertie,' said Claude. 'A sportsman to the finger-tips. Well, has Bingo told you about it?'

'Not a word. He's been——'

'We've been talking,' said Bingo hastily, 'of other matters.'

Claude pinched the last slice of thin bread-and-butter, and Eustace poured himself out a cup of tea.

'It's like this, Bertie,' said Eustace, settling down cosily. 'As I told you in my letter, there are nine of us marooned in this desert spot, reading with old Heppenstall. Well, of course, nothing is jollier than sweating up the Classics when it's a hundred in the shade, but there does come a time when you begin to feel the need of a little relaxation; and, by Jove, there are absolutely no facilities for relaxation in this place whatever. And then Steggles got this idea. Steggles is one of our reading-party, and, between ourselves, rather a worm as a general thing. Still, you have to give him credit for getting this idea.'

'What idea?'

'Well, you know how many parsons there are round about here. There are about a dozen hamlets within a radius of six miles, and each hamlet has a church and each church has a parson and each parson preaches a sermon every Sunday. Tomorrow week — Sunday the twenty-third — we're running off the great Sermon Handicap. Steggles is making the book. Each parson is to be clocked by a reliable steward of the course, and the one that preaches the longest sermon wins. Did you study the race-card I sent you?'

'I couldn't understand what it was all about.'

'Why, you chump, it gives the handicaps and the current odds on each starter. I've got another one here, in case you've lost yours. Take a careful look at it. It gives you the thing in a nutshell. Jeeves, old son, do you want a sporting flutter?'

'Sir?' said Jeeves, who had just meandered in with my breakfast.

Claude explained the scheme. Amazing the way Jeeves grasped it right off. But he merely smiled in a paternal sort of way.

'Thank you, sir, I think not.'

'Well, you're with us, Bertie, aren't you?' said Claude, sneaking a roll and a slice of bacon. 'Have you studied that card? Well, tell me, does anything strike you about it?'

Of course it did. It had struck me the moment I looked at it.

'Why, it's a sitter for old Heppenstall,' I said. 'He's got the event sewed up in a parcel. There isn't a parson in the land who could give him eight minutes. Your pal Steggles must be an ass, giving him a handicap like that. Why, in the days when I was with him, old Heppenstall never used to preach under half an hour, and there was one sermon of his on Brotherly Love which lasted forty-five minutes if it lasted a second. Has he lost his vim lately, or what is it?'

'Not a bit of it,' said Eustace. 'Tell him what happened, Claude.'

'Why,' said Claude, 'the first Sunday we were here, we all went to Twing church, and old Heppenstall preached a sermon that was well under twenty minutes. This is what happened. Steggles didn't notice it, and the Rev. didn't notice it himself, but Eustace and I both spotted that he had dropped a chunk of at least half a dozen pages out of his sermon-case as he was walking up to the pulpit. He sort of flickered when he got to the gap in the manuscript, but carried on all right, and Steggles went away with the impression that twenty minutes or a bit under was his usual form. The next Sunday we heard Tucker and Starkie, and they both went well over the thirty-five minutes, so Steggles arranged the handicapping as you see on the card. You must come into this, Bertie. You see, the trouble is that I haven't a bean, and Eustace hasn't a bean, and Bingo Little hasn't a bean, so you'll have to finance the syndicate. Don't weaken! It's just putting money in all our pockets. Well, we'll have to be getting back now. Think the thing over, and phone me later in the day. And, if you let us down, Bertie, may a cousin's curse— Come on, Claude, old thing.'

The more I studied the scheme, the better it looked.

'How about it, Jeeves?' I said.

Jeeves smiled gently, and drifted out.

'Jeeves has no sporting blood,' said Bingo.

'Well, I have. I'm coming into this. Claude's quite right. It's like finding money by the wayside.'

'Good man!' said Bingo. 'Now I can see daylight. Say I have a tenner on Heppenstall, and cop; that'll give me a bit in hand to back Pink Pill with in the two o'clock at Gatwick the week after next: cop on that, put the pile on Musk-Rat for the one-thirty at Lewes, and there I am with a nice little sum to take to Alexandra Park on September the tenth, when I've got a tip straight from the stable.'

It sounded like a bit out of *Smiles's Self-Help*.

'And then,' said young Bingo, 'I'll be in a position to go to my uncle and beard him in his lair somewhat. He's quite a bit of a snob, you know, and when he hears that I'm going to marry the daughter of an earl—'

'I say, old man,' I couldn't help saying, 'aren't you looking ahead rather far?'

'Oh, that's all right. It's true nothing's actually settled yet, but she practically told me the other day she was fond of me.'

'What!'

'Well, she said that the sort of man she liked was the self-reliant, manly man with strength, good looks, character, ambition, and initiative.'

'Leave me, laddie,' I said. 'Leave me to my fried egg.'

Directly I'd got up I went to the phone, snatched Eustace away from his morning's work, and instructed him to put a tenner on the Twing flier at current odds for each of the syndicate; and after lunch Eustace rang me up to say that he had done business at a snappy seven-to-one, the odds having lengthened owing to a rumour in knowledgeable circles that the Rev. was subject to hay-fever, and was taking big chances strolling in the paddock behind the Vicarage in the early mornings. And it was dashed lucky, I thought next day, that we had managed to get the money on in time, for on the Sunday morning old Heppenstall fairly took the bit between his teeth, and gave us thirty-six solid minutes on Certain Popular Superstitions. I was sitting next to Steggles in the pew, and I saw him blench visibly. He was a little rat-faced fellow, with shifty eyes and a suspicious nature. The first thing he did when we emerged into the open air was to announce, formally,

that anyone who fancied the Rev. could now be accom-
modated at fifteen-to-eight on, and he added, in a
rather nasty manner, that if he had his way, this sort of
in-and-out running would be brought to the attention
of the Jockey Club, but that he supposed that there was
nothing to be done about it. This ruinous price checked
the punters at once, and there was little money in sight.
And so matters stood till just after lunch on Tuesday
afternoon, when, as I was strolling up and down in
front of the house with a cigarette, Claude and Eustace
came bursting up the drive on bicycles, dripping with
momentous news.

'Bertie,' said Claude, deeply agitated, 'unless we
take immediate action and do a bit of quick thinking,
we're in the cart.'

'What's the matter?'

'G. Hayward's the matter,' said Eustace morosely.
'The Lower Bingley starter.'

'We never even considered him,' said Claude.
'Somehow or other, he got overlooked. It's always
the way. Steggles overlooked him. We all overlooked
him. But Eustace and I happened by the merest fluke
to be riding through Lower Bingley this morning,
and there was a wedding on at the church, and it suddenly struck us that it wouldn't be a bad move to get a
line on G. Hayward's form, in case he might be a dark
horse.'

'And it was jolly lucky we did,' said Eustace. 'He
delivered an address of twenty-six minutes by Claude's

stop-watch. At a village wedding, mark you! What'll he do when he really extends himself!'

'There's only one thing to be done, Bertie,' said Claude. 'You must spring some more funds, so that we can hedge on Hayward and save ourselves.'

'But—'

'Well, it's the only way out.'

'But I say, you know, I hate the idea of all that money we put on Heppenstall being chucked away.'

'What else can you suggest? You don't suppose the Rev. can give this absolute marvel a handicap and win, do you?'

'I've got it!' I said.

'What?'

'I see a way by which we can make it safe for our nominee. I'll pop over this afternoon, and ask him as a personal favour to preach that sermon of his on Brotherly Love on Sunday.'

Claude and Eustace looked at each other, like those chappies in the poem, with a wild surmise.

'It's a scheme,' said Claude.

'A jolly brainy scheme,' said Eustace. 'I didn't think you had it in you, Bertie.'

'But even so,' said Claude, 'fizzer as that sermon no doubt is, will it be good enough in the face of a four-minute handicap?'

'Rather!' I said. 'When I told you it lasted forty-five minutes, I was probably understating it. I should call it – from my recollection of the thing – nearer fifty.'

'Then carry on,' said Claude.

I toddled over in the evening and fixed the thing up. Old Heppenstall was most decent about the whole affair. He seemed pleased and touched that I should have remembered the sermon all these years, and said he had once or twice had an idea of preaching it again, only it had seemed to him, on reflection, that it was perhaps a trifle long for a rustic congregation.

'And in these restless times, my dear Wooster,' he said, 'I fear that brevity in the pulpit is becoming more and more desiderated by even the bucolic churchgoer, who one might have supposed would be less afflicted with the spirit of hurry and impatience than his metropolitan brother. I have had many arguments on the subject with my nephew, young Bates, who is taking my old friend Spettigue's cure over at Gandle-by-the-Hill. His view is that a sermon nowadays should be a bright, brisk, straight-from-the-shoulder address, never lasting more than ten or twelve minutes.'

'Long?' I said. 'Why, my goodness! you don't call that Brotherly Love sermon of yours *long*, do you?'

'It takes fully fifty minutes to deliver.'

'Surely not?'

'Your incredulity, my dear Wooster, is extremely flattering – far more flattering, of course, than I deserve. Nevertheless, the facts are as I have stated. You are sure that I would not be well advised to make certain excisions and eliminations? You do not think it would be a good thing to cut, to prune? I might, for example, delete the rather exhaustive excursus into the family life of the early Assyrians?'

'Don't touch a word of it, or you'll spoil the whole thing,' I said earnestly.

'I am delighted to hear you say so, and I shall preach the sermon without fail next Sunday morning.'

What I have always said, and what I always shall say, is, that this ante-post betting is a mistake, an error, and a mug's game. You never can tell what's going to happen. If fellows would only stick to the good old S.P. there would be fewer young men go wrong. I'd hardly finished my breakfast on the Saturday morning, when Jeeves came to my bedside to say that Eustace wanted me on the telephone.

'Good Lord, Jeeves, what's the matter, do you think?'

I'm bound to say I was beginning to get a bit jumpy by this time.

'Mr Eustace did not confide in me, sir.'

'Has he got the wind up?'

'Somewhat vertically, sir, to judge by his voice.'

'Do you know what I think, Jeeves? Something's gone wrong with the favourite.'

'Which is the favourite, sir?'

'Mr Heppenstall. He's gone to odds on. He was intending to preach a sermon on Brotherly Love which would have brought him home by lengths. I wonder if anything's happened to him.'

'You could ascertain, sir, by speaking to Mr Eustace on the telephone. He is holding the wire.'

'By Jove, yes!'

I shoved on a dressing-gown, and flew downstairs like a mighty, rushing wind. The moment I heard Eustace's voice I knew we were for it. It had a croak of agony in it.

'Bertie?'

'Here I am.'

'Deuce of a time you've been. Bertie, we're sunk. The favourite's blown up.'

'No!'

'Yes. Coughing in his stable all last night.'

'What!'

'Absolutely! Hay-fever.'

'Oh, my sainted aunt!'

'The doctor is with him now, and it's only a question of minutes before he's officially scratched. That means the curate will show up at the post instead, and he's no good at all. He is being offered at a hundred-to-six, but no takers. What shall we do?'

I had to grapple with the thing for a moment in silence.

'Eustace.'

'Hallo?'

'What can you get on G. Hayward?'

'Only four to one now. I think there's been a leak, and Steggles has heard something. The odds shortened late last night in a significant manner.'

'Well, four to one will clear us. Put another fiver all round on G. Hayward for the syndicate. That'll bring us out on the right side of the ledger.'

'If he wins.'

'What do you mean? I thought you considered him a cert., bar Heppenstall.'

'I'm beginning to wonder,' said Eustace gloomily, 'if there's such a thing as a cert. in this world. I'm told the Rev. Joseph Tucker did an extraordinarily fine trial gallop at a mothers' meeting over at Badgwick yesterday. However, it seems our only chance. So-long.'

Not being one of the official stewards, I had my choice of churches next morning, and naturally I didn't hesitate. The only drawback to going to Lower Bingley was that it was ten miles away, which meant an early start, but I borrowed a bicycle from one of the grooms and tooled off. I had only Eustace's word for it that G. Hayward was such a stayer, and it might have been that he had showed too flattering form at that wedding where the twins had heard him preach; but any misgivings I may have had disappeared the moment he got into the pulpit. Eustace had been right. The man was a trier. He was a tall, rangy-looking greybeard, and he went off from the start with a nice, easy action, pausing and clearing his throat at the end of each sentence, and it wasn't five minutes before I realized that here was the winner. His habit of stopping dead and looking round the church at intervals was worth minutes to us, and in the home stretch we gained no little advantage owing to his dropping his pince-nez and having to grope for them. At the twenty-minute mark he had merely settled down. Twenty-five minutes saw him going strong. And when he finally finished with a good burst, the clock showed thirty-five minutes fourteen seconds. With the handicap which he had been given, this seemed to me to make the event easy for him, and it was with much *bonhomie* and goodwill to all men that I hopped on to the old bike and started back to the Hall for lunch.

Bingo was talking on the phone when I arrived.

'Fine! Splendid! Topping!' he was saying. 'Eh? Oh, we needn't worry about him. Right-o, I'll tell Bertie.' He hung up the receiver and caught sight of me. 'Oh, hallo, Bertie; I was just talking to Eustace. It's all right, old man. The report from Lower Bingley has just got in. G. Hayward romps home.'

'I knew he would. I've just come from there.'

'Oh, were you there? I went to Badgwick. Tucker ran a splendid race, but the handicap was too much for him. Starkie had a sore throat and was nowhere. Roberts, of Fale-by-the-Water, ran third. Good old G. Hayward!' said Bingo affectionately, and we strolled out on to the terrace.

'Are all the returns in, then?' I asked.

'All except Gandle-by-the-Hill. But we needn't worry about Bates. He never had a chance. By the way, poor old Jeeves loses his tenner. Silly ass!'

'Jeeves? How do you mean?'

'He came to me this morning, just after you had left, and asked me to put a tenner on Bates for him. I told him he was a chump, and begged him not to throw his money away, but he would do it.'

'I beg your pardon, sir. This note arrived for you just after you had left the house this morning.'

Jeeves had materialized from nowhere, and was standing at my elbow.

'Eh? What? Note?'

'The Reverend Mr Heppenstall's butler brought it over from the Vicarage, sir. It came too late to be delivered to you at the moment.'

Young Bingo was talking to Jeeves like a father on the subject of betting against the form-book. The yell I gave made him bite his tongue in the middle of a sentence.

'What the dickens is the matter?' he asked, not a little peeved.

'We're dished! Listen to this!'

I read him the note:

> The Vicarage,
> Twing, Glos.

MY DEAR WOOSTER — As you may have heard, circumstances over which I have no control will prevent my preaching the sermon on Brotherly Love for which you made such a flattering request. I am unwilling, however, that you shall be disappointed, so, if you will attend divine service at Gandle-by-the-Hill this morning, you will hear my sermon preached by young Bates, my nephew. I have lent him the manuscript at his urgent desire, for, between ourselves, there are wheels within wheels. My nephew is one of the candidates for the headmastership of a well-known public school, and the choice has narrowed down between him and one rival.

Late yesterday evening James received private information that the head of the Board of Governors of the school proposed to sit under him this Sunday in order to judge of the merits of his preaching, a most important item in swaying the Board's choice. I acceded to his plea that I lend him my sermon on Brotherly Love, of which, like you, he apparently retains a vivid recollection. It would have been too late for him to compose a sermon of suitable length in place of the brief address which – mistakenly, in my opinion – he had designed to deliver to his rustic flock, and I wished to help the boy.

Trusting that his preaching of the sermon will supply you with as pleasant memories as you say you have of mine, I remain,

Cordially yours,

F. Heppenstall.

P.S. – The hay-fever has rendered my eyes unpleasantly weak for the time being, so I am dictating this letter to my butler, Brookfield, who will convey it to you.

I don't know when I've experienced a more massive silence than the one that followed my reading of this cheery epistle. Young Bingo gulped once or twice, and practically every known emotion came and went on his face. Jeeves coughed one soft, low, gentle cough like a sheep with a blade of grass stuck in its throat, and then stood gazing serenely at the landscape. Finally young Bingo spoke.

'Great Scott!' he whispered hoarsely. 'An S.P. job!'

'I believe that is the technical term, sir,' said Jeeves.

'So you had inside information, dash it!' said young Bingo.

'Why, yes, sir,' said Jeeves. 'Brookfield happened to mention the contents of the note to me when he brought it. We are old friends.'

Bingo registered grief, anguish, rage, despair and resentment.

'Well, all I can say,' he cried, 'is that it's a bit thick! Preaching another man's sermon! Do you call that honest? Do you call that playing the game?'

'Well, my dear old thing,' I said, 'be fair. It's quite within the rules. Clergymen do it all the time. They aren't expected always to make up the sermons they preach.'

Jeeves coughed again, and fixed me with an expressionless eye.

'And in the present case, sir, if I may be permitted to take the liberty of making the observation, I think we should make allowances. We should remember that the securing of this headmastership meant everything to the young couple.'

'Young couple? What young couple?'

'The Reverend James Bates, sir, and Lady Cynthia. I am informed by her ladyship's maid that they have been engaged to be married for some weeks – provisionally, so to speak; and his lordship made his consent conditional on Mr Bates securing a really important and remunerative position.'

Young Bingo turned a light green.

'Engaged to be married!'

'Yes, sir.'

There was a silence.

'I think I'll go for a walk,' said Bingo.

'But, my dear old thing,' I said, 'it's just lunch-time. The gong will be going any minute now.'

'I don't want any lunch!' said Bingo.

PELHAM GRENVILLE WODEHOUSE (always known as 'Plum') wrote more than ninety novels and some three hundred short stories over 73 years. He is widely recognised as the greatest 20th-century writer of humour in the English language.

Perhaps best known for the escapades of Bertie Wooster and Jeeves, Wodehouse also created the world of Blandings Castle, home to Lord Emsworth and his cherished pig, the Empress of Blandings. His stories include gems concerning the irrepressible and disreputable Ukridge; Psmith, the elegant socialist; the ever-so-slightly-unscrupulous Fifth Earl of Ickenham, better known as Uncle Fred; and those related by Mr Mulliner, the charming raconteur of The Angler's Rest, and the Oldest Member at the Golf Club.

In 1936 he was awarded the Mark Twain Prize for 'having made an outstanding and lasting contribution to the happiness of the world'. He was made a Doctor of Letters by Oxford University in 1939 and in 1975, aged 93, he was knighted by Queen Elizabeth II. He died shortly afterwards, on St Valentine's Day.

# ALSO AVAILABLE IN THIS SERIES

Featuring

*The Amazing Hat Mystery*

*Uncle Fred Flits By*

*Trouble Down at Tudsleigh*

Featuring

*Goodbye to All Cats*

*Ukridge's Dog College*

*Ukridge's Accident Syndicate*

Featuring

*Mulliner's Buck-U-Uppo*

*The Spot of Art*

*Strychnine in the Soup*